VADER DOWN: VOLUME 6

It is a period of unrest. Darth Vader has tracked his son, the rebel pilot Luke Skywalker, to the planet Vrogas Vas. The pair crash-landed, only to be stranded planetside and faced with new enemies.

After Han and Chewie rescued Luke from Dr. Aphra's hold, they now find themselves locked in a dangerous and deadly battle with Wookiee warrior Black Krrsantan.

Meanwhile, Luke has gone to find Princess Leia, who had ordered all rebel forces to strike on Darth Vader's location. However, Luke soon found himself captured by Imperial forces led by the Mon Calamari cyborg, Commander Karbin, who had tracked the Sith Lord to the planet to end both Vader and the Rebels in one fell swoop....

KIERON GILLEN
Writer

SALVADOR LARROCA
Artist

EDGAR DELGADO
Colorist

**JASON AARON &
KIERON GILLEN**
Story

VC's JOE CARAMAGNA
Letterer

MARK BROOKS
Cover Artist

HEATHER ANTOS
Assistant Editor

JORDAN D. WHITE
Editor

**C.B.
CEBULSKI**
Executive Editor

**AXEL
ALONSO**
Editor In Chief

**JOE
QUESADA**
Chief Creative Officer

**DAN
BUCKLEY**
Publisher

For Lucasfilm:
Senior Editor FRANK PARISI
Creative Director MICHAEL SIGLAIN
Lucasfilm Story Group RAYNE ROBERTS, PABLO HIDALGO,
LELAND CHEE

ABDO
Spotlight

ABDOPUBLISHING.COM

Reinforced library bound edition published in 2017 by Spotlight,
a division of ABDO, PO Box 398166, Minneapolis, Minnesota 55439.
Spotlight produces high-quality reinforced library bound editions for
schools and libraries. Published by agreement with Marvel Characters, Inc.

Printed in the United States of America, North Mankato, Minnesota.
092016
012017

 THIS BOOK CONTAINS
RECYCLED MATERIALS

STAR WARS © & TM 2016 LUCASFILM LTD.

PUBLISHER'S CATALOGING IN PUBLICATION DATA

Names: Aaron, Jason ; Gillen, Kieron authors. | Deodato, Mike ; Martin, Laura ;
Larroca, Salvador ; Delgado, Edgar, illustrators.
Title: Vader Down / writers: Jason Aaron ; Kieron Gillen ; art: Mike Deodato;
Laura Martin ; Salvador Larroca ; Edgar Delgado.
Description: Reinforced library bound edition. | Minneapolis, Minnesota : Spotlight,
2017. | Series: Star Wars : Vader Down
Summary: Darth Vader tracks Luke Skywalker's location to Vrogas Vas, but when
they're stranded on the planet, they face new enemies and challenges.
Identifiers: LCCN 2016941801 | ISBN 9781614795612 (volume 1) | ISBN
9781614795629 (volume 2) | ISBN 9781614795636 (volume 3) | ISBN
9781614795643 (volume 4) | ISBN 9781614795650 (volume 5) | ISBN
9781614795667 (volume 6)
Subjects: LCSH: Vader, Darth (Fictitious character)--Juvenile fiction. | Star Wars
fiction--Comic books, strips, etc.--Juvenile fiction. | Graphic novels--Juvenile
fiction.
Classification: DDC 741.5--dc23
LC record available at https://lccn.loc.gov/2016941801

Spotlight

A Division of ABDO
abdopublishing.com

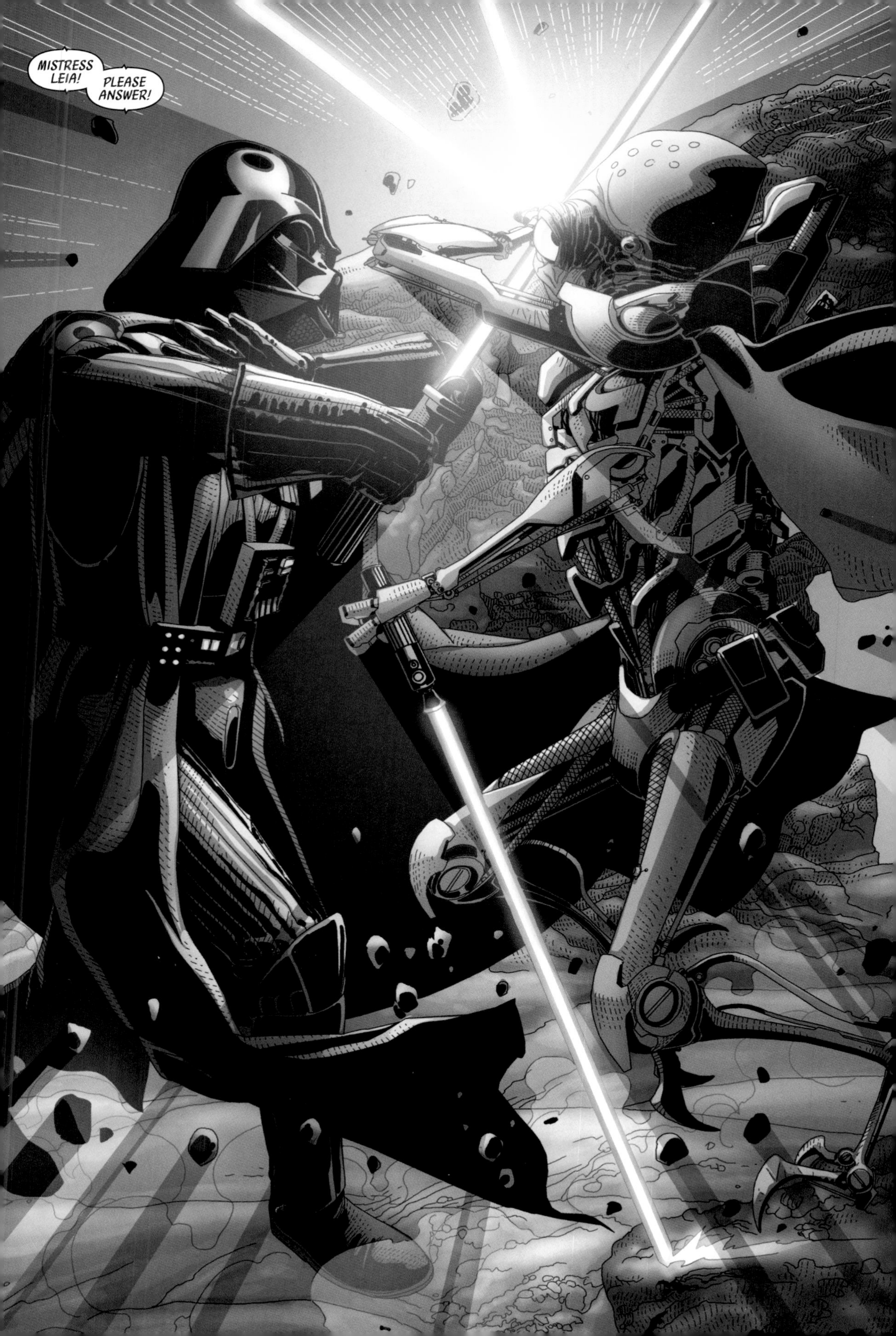
MISTRESS LEIA!
PLEASE ANSWER!

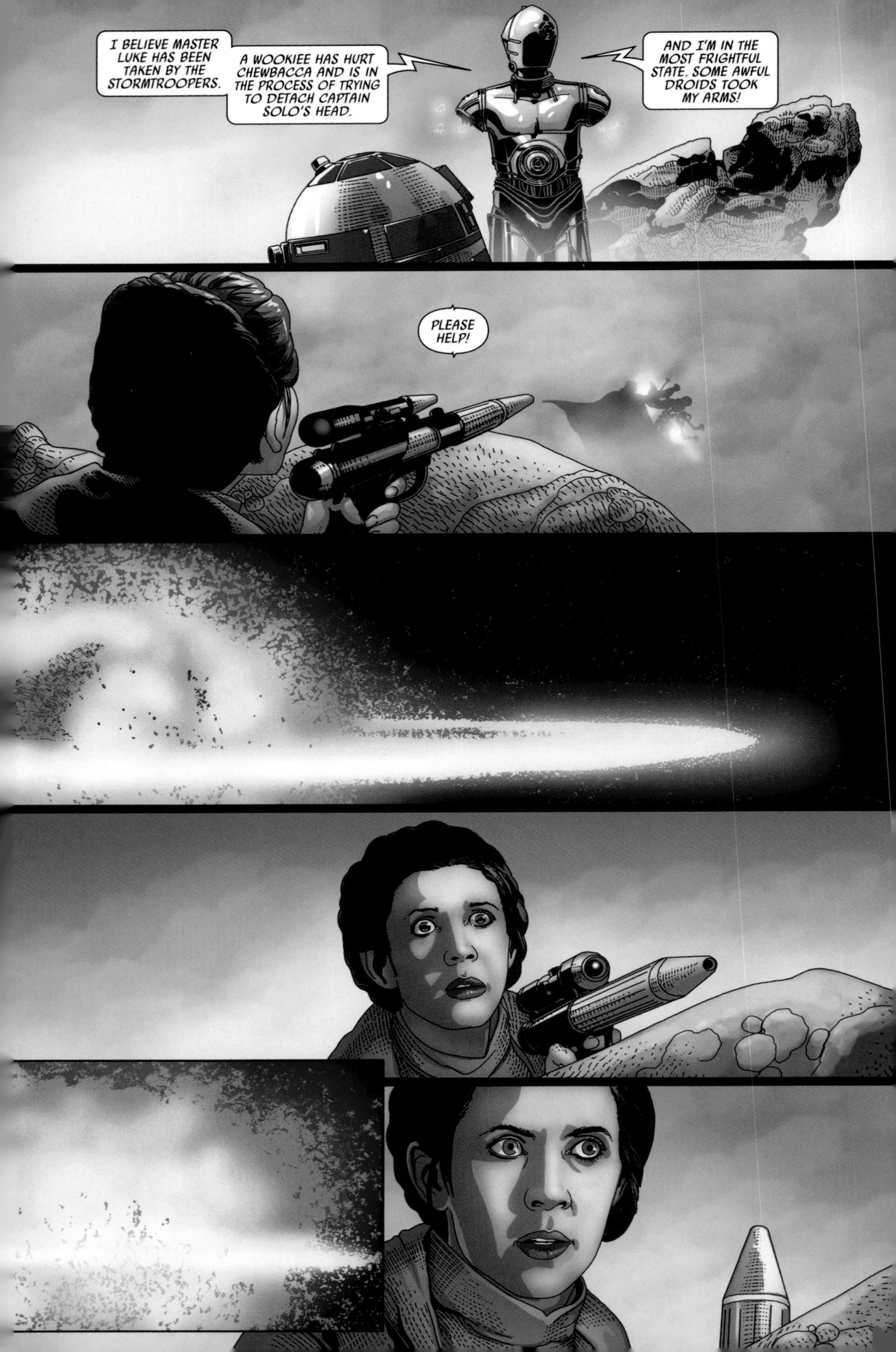
I BELIEVE MASTER LUKE HAS BEEN TAKEN BY THE STORMTROOPERS.
A WOOKIEE HAS HURT CHEWBACCA AND IS IN THE PROCESS OF TRYING TO DETACH CAPTAIN SOLO'S HEAD.
AND I'M IN THE MOST FRIGHTFUL STATE. SOME AWFUL DROIDS TOOK MY ARMS!
PLEASE HELP!

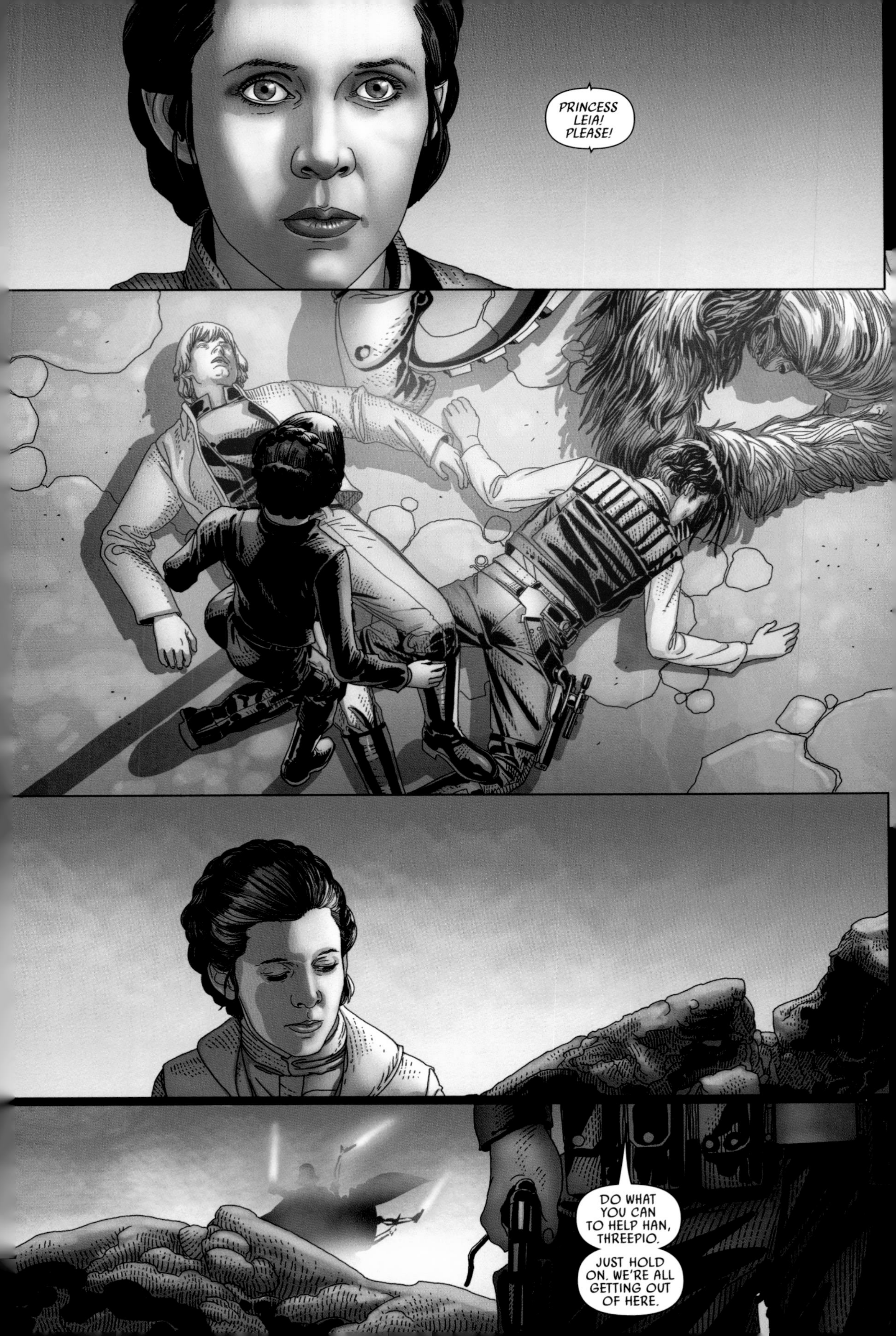
PRINCESS LEIA! PLEASE!
DO WHAT YOU CAN TO HELP HAN, THREEPIO.
JUST HOLD ON. WE'RE ALL GETTING OUT OF HERE.

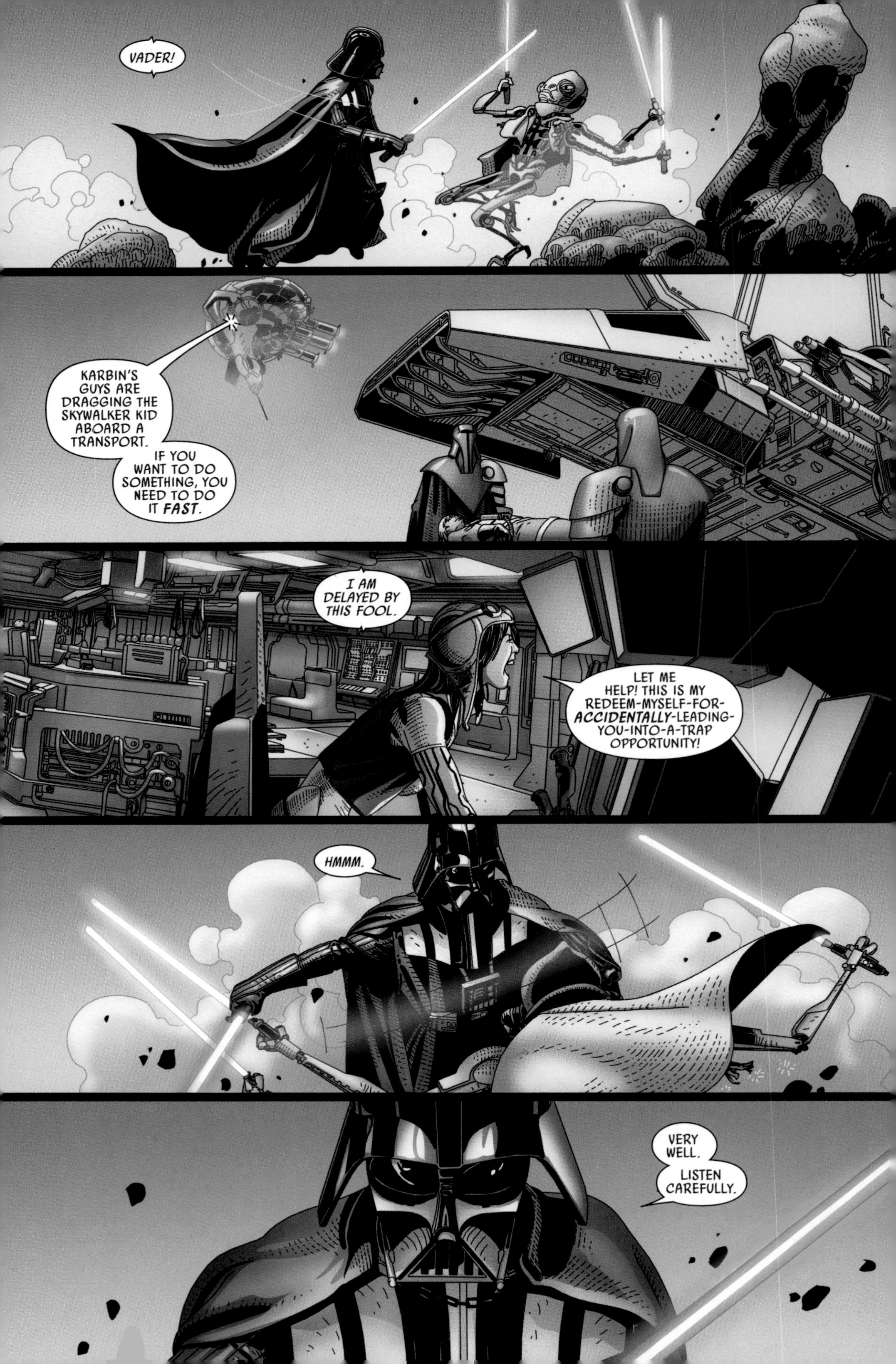

VADER!
KARBIN'S GUYS ARE DRAGGING THE SKYWALKER KID ABOARD A TRANSPORT.
IF YOU WANT TO DO SOMETHING, YOU NEED TO DO IT FAST.
I AM DELAYED BY THIS FOOL.
LET ME HELP! THIS IS MY REDEEM-MYSELF-FOR-ACCIDENTALLY-LEADING-YOU-INTO-A-TRAP OPPORTUNITY!
HMMM.
VERY WELL.
LISTEN CAREFULLY.

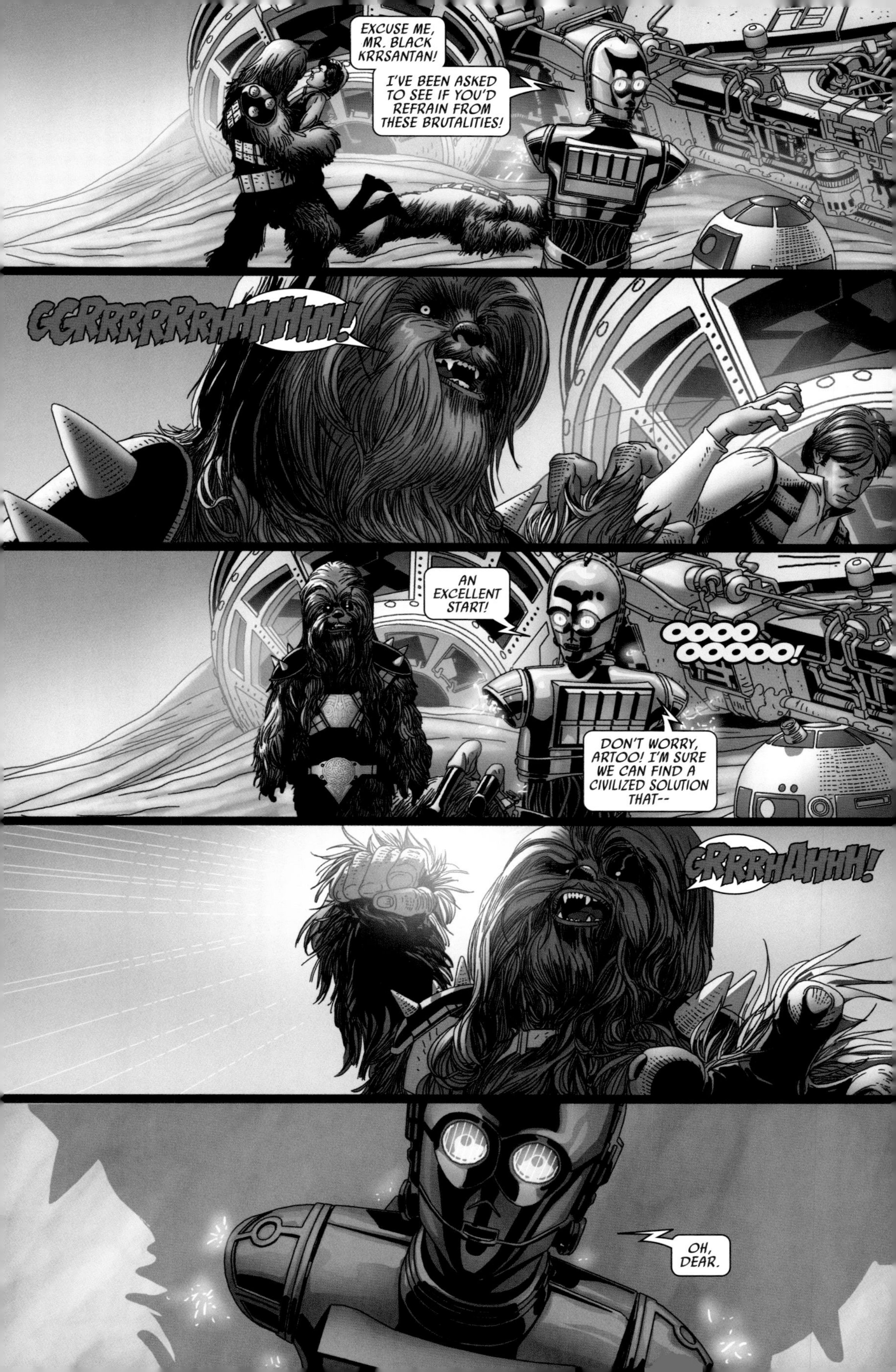
EXCUSE ME, MR. BLACK KRRSANTAN!
I'VE BEEN ASKED TO SEE IF YOU'D REFRAIN FROM THESE BRUTALITIES!
GGRRRRRRHHHHHH!
AN EXCELLENT START!
OOOO OOOOO!
DON'T WORRY, ARTOO! I'M SURE WE CAN FIND A CIVILIZED SOLUTION THAT--
GRRRHAHHH!
OH, DEAR.

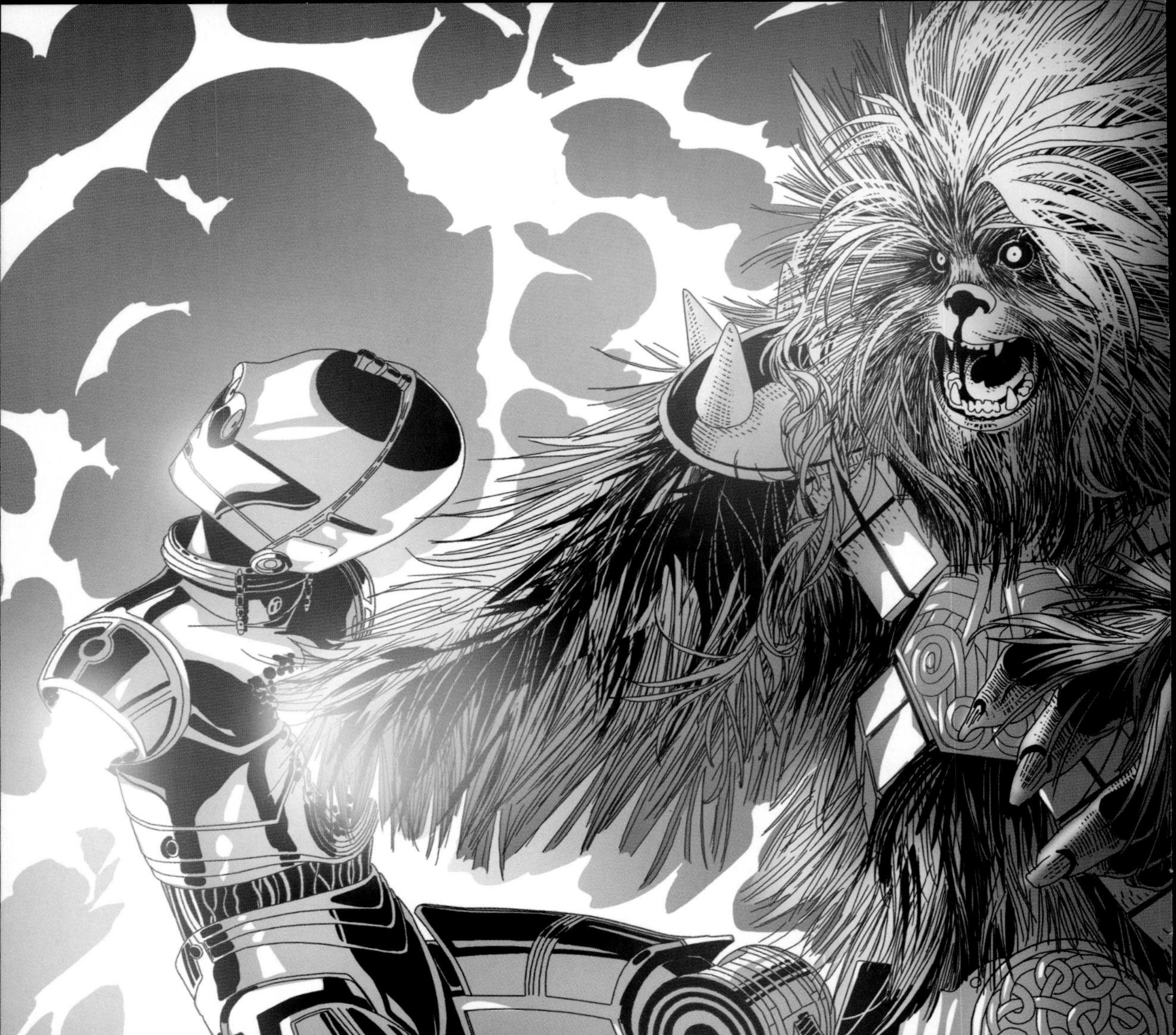

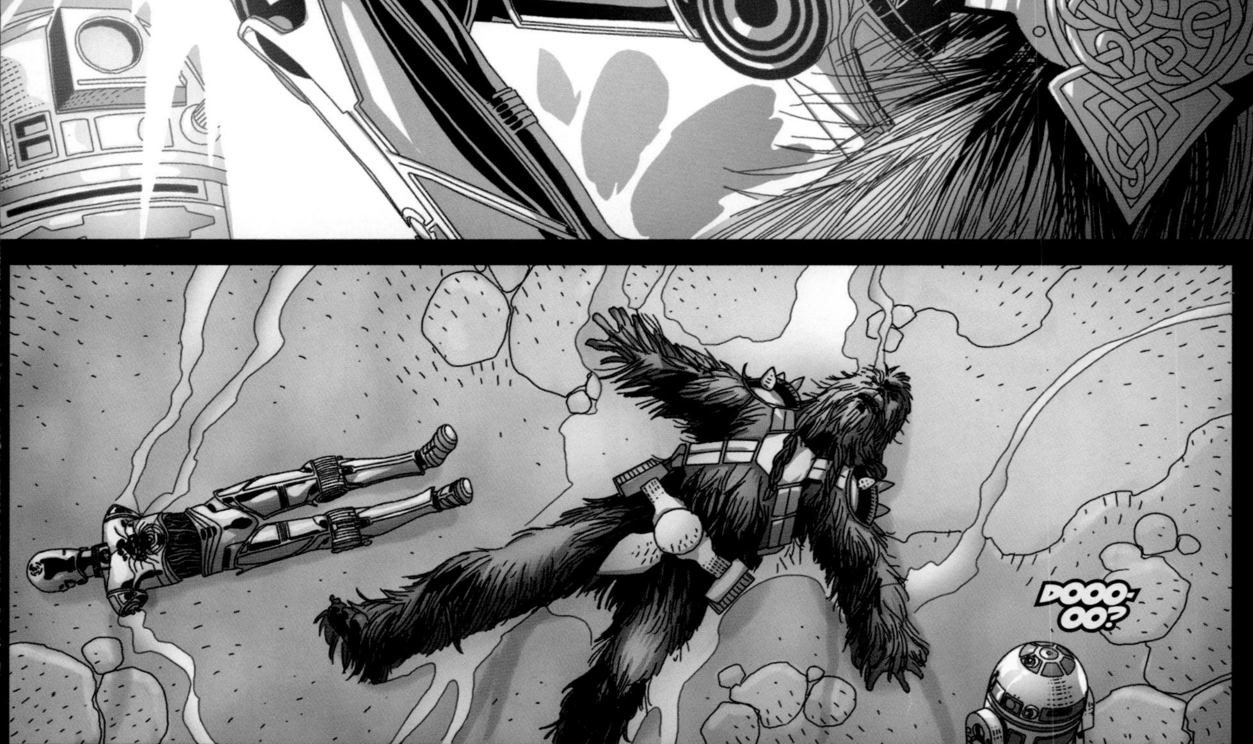
DOOO-OO?

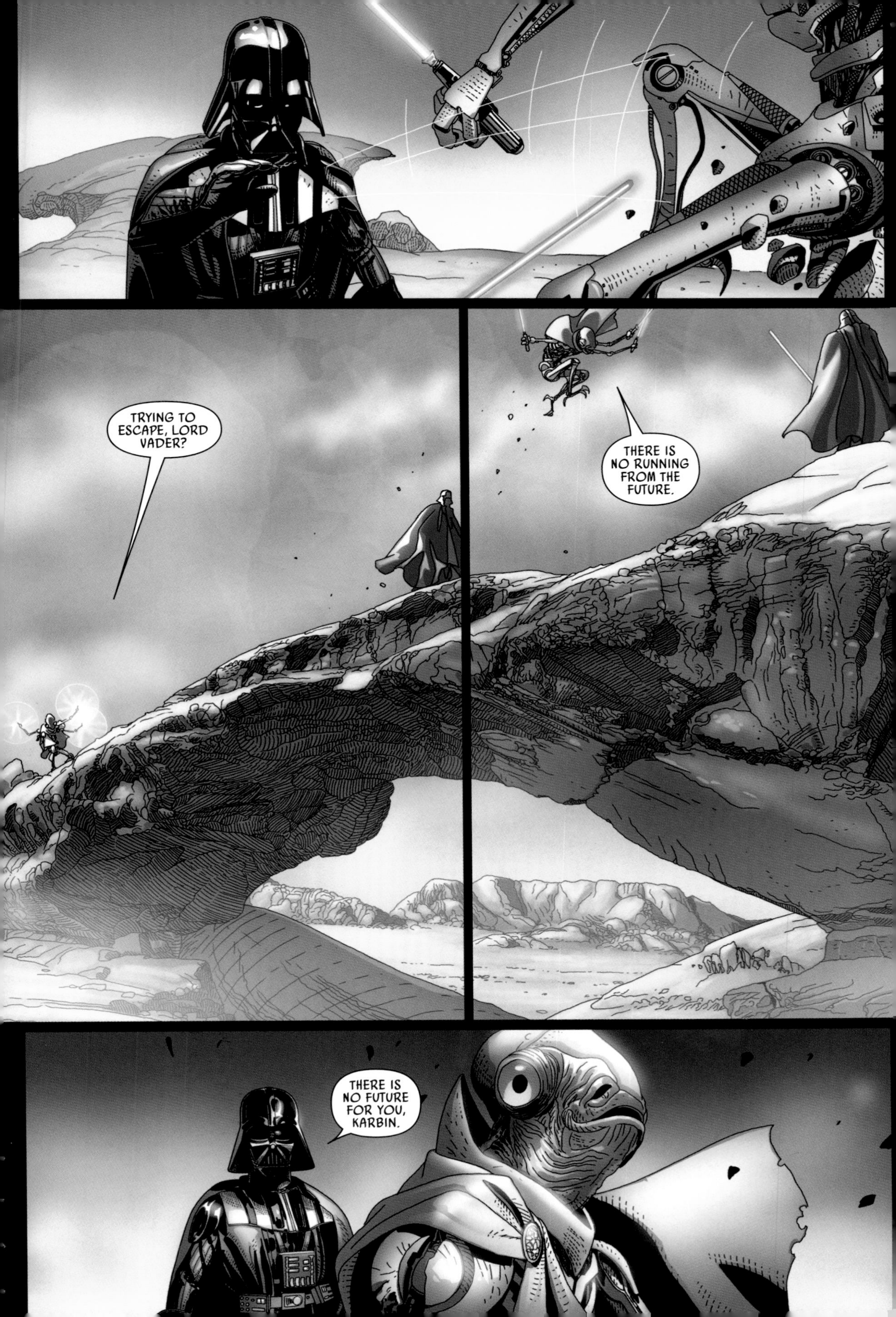
TRYING TO ESCAPE, LORD VADER?
THERE IS NO RUNNING FROM THE FUTURE.
THERE IS NO FUTURE FOR YOU, KARBIN.

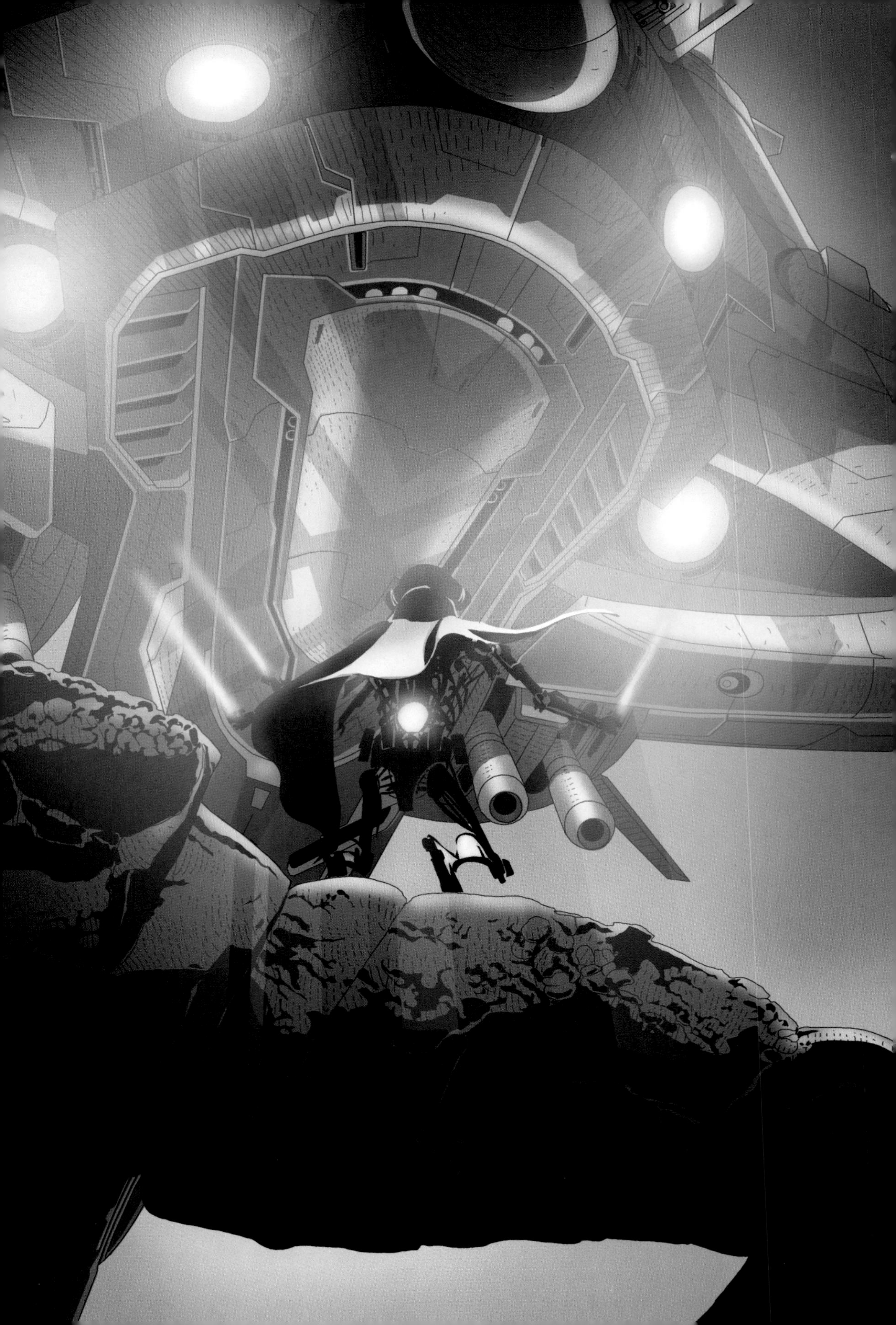

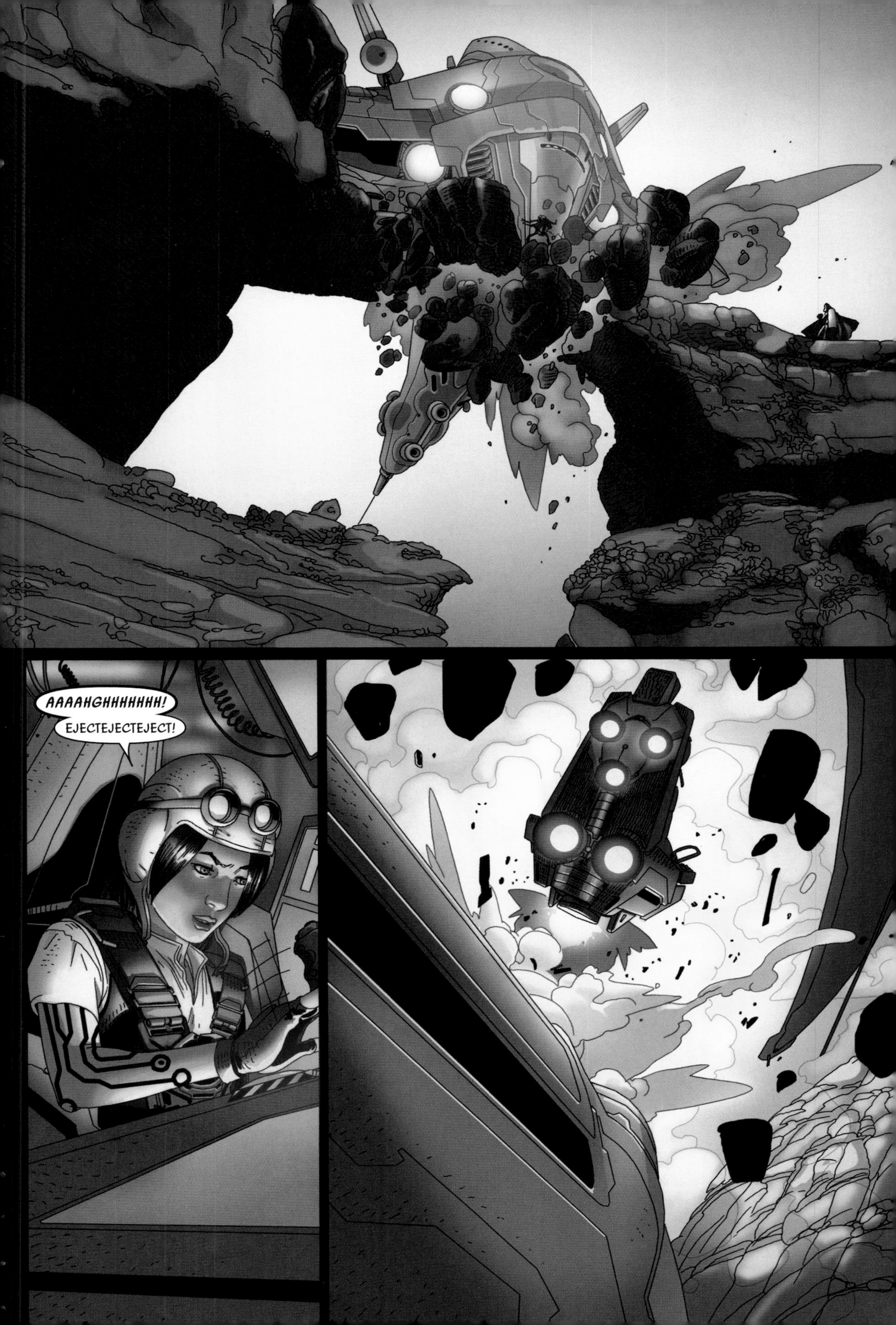
AAAAHGHHHHHHH!
EJECTEJECTEJECT!

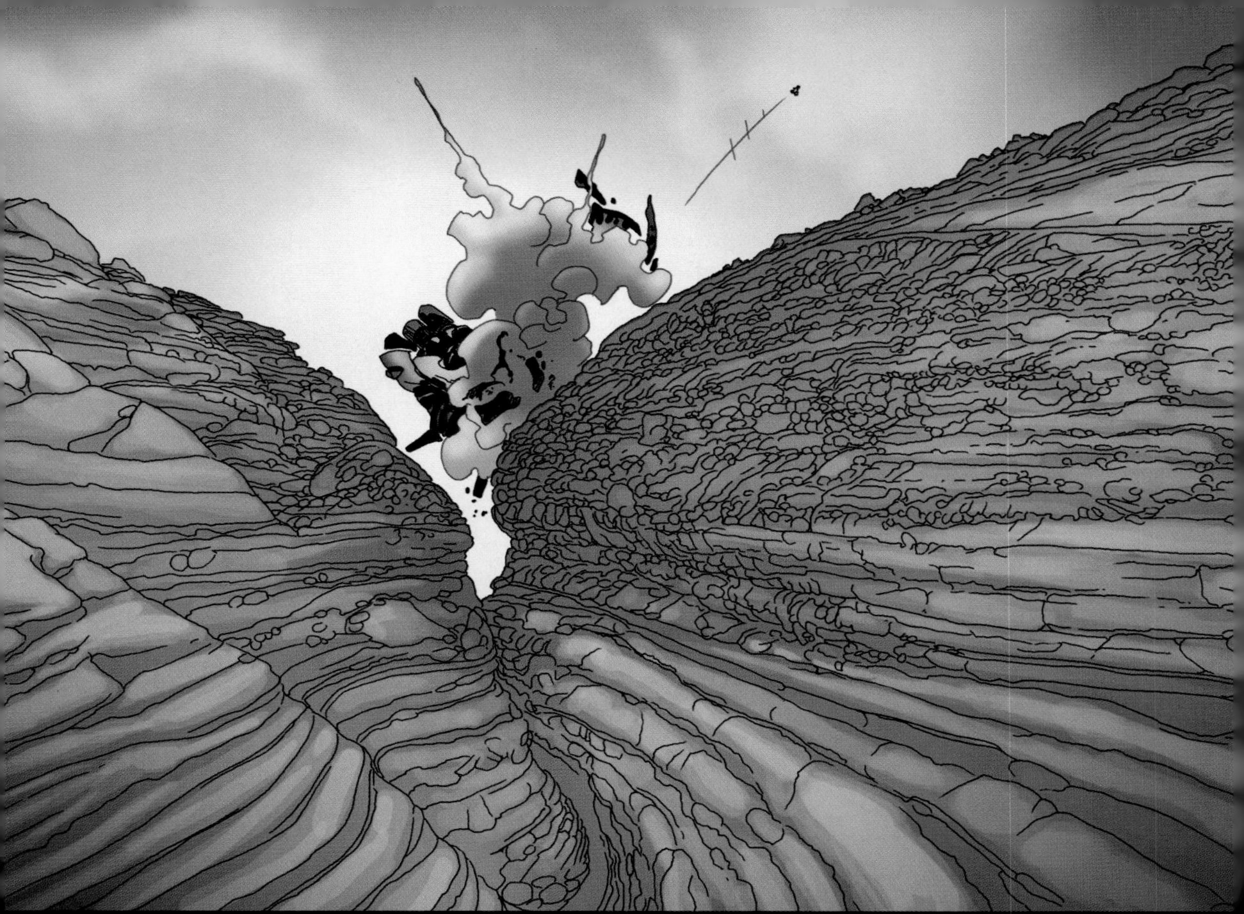
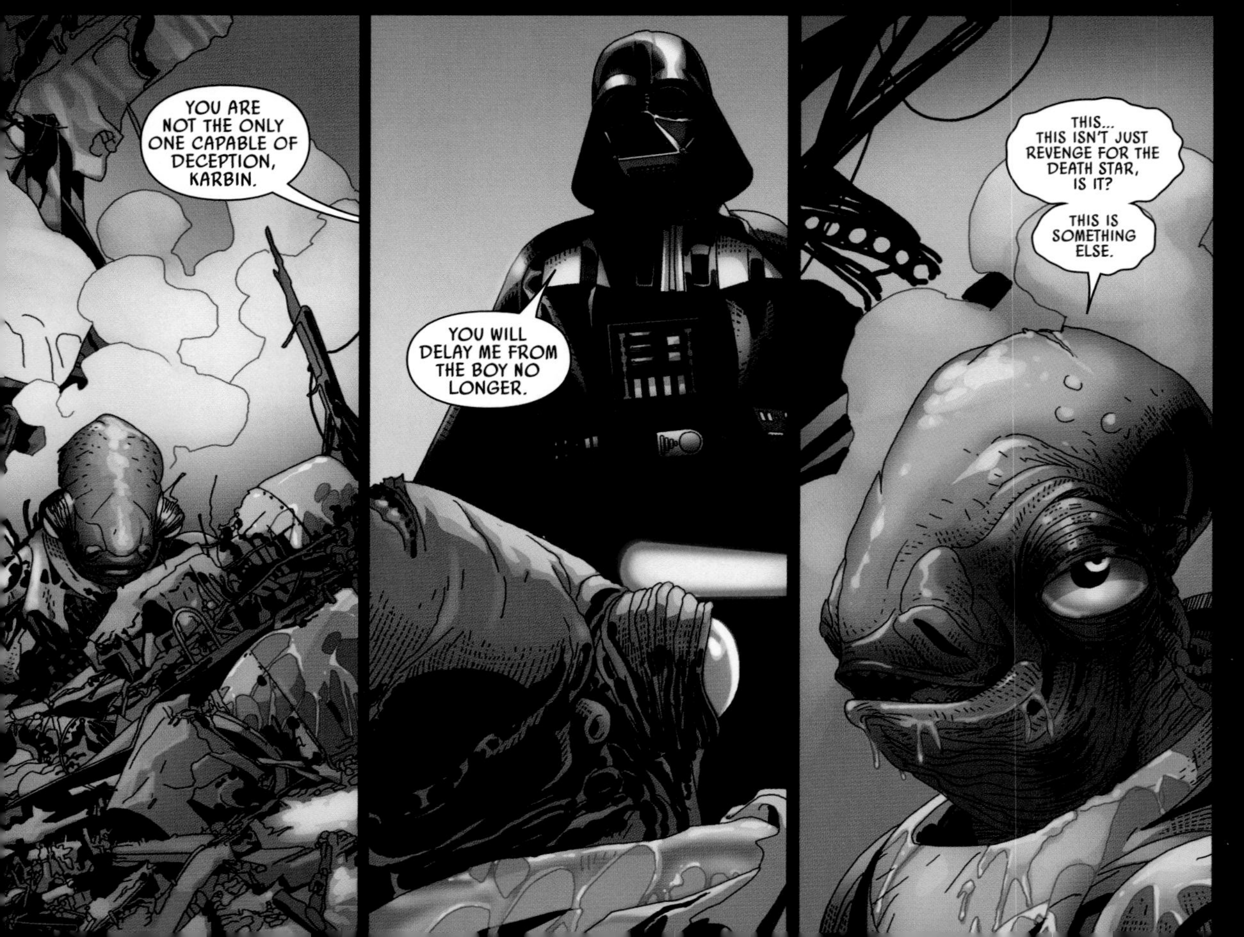
YOU ARE NOT THE ONLY ONE CAPABLE OF DECEPTION, KARBIN.
YOU WILL DELAY ME FROM THE BOY NO LONGER.
THIS... THIS ISN'T JUST REVENGE FOR THE DEATH STAR, IS IT?
THIS IS SOMETHING ELSE.

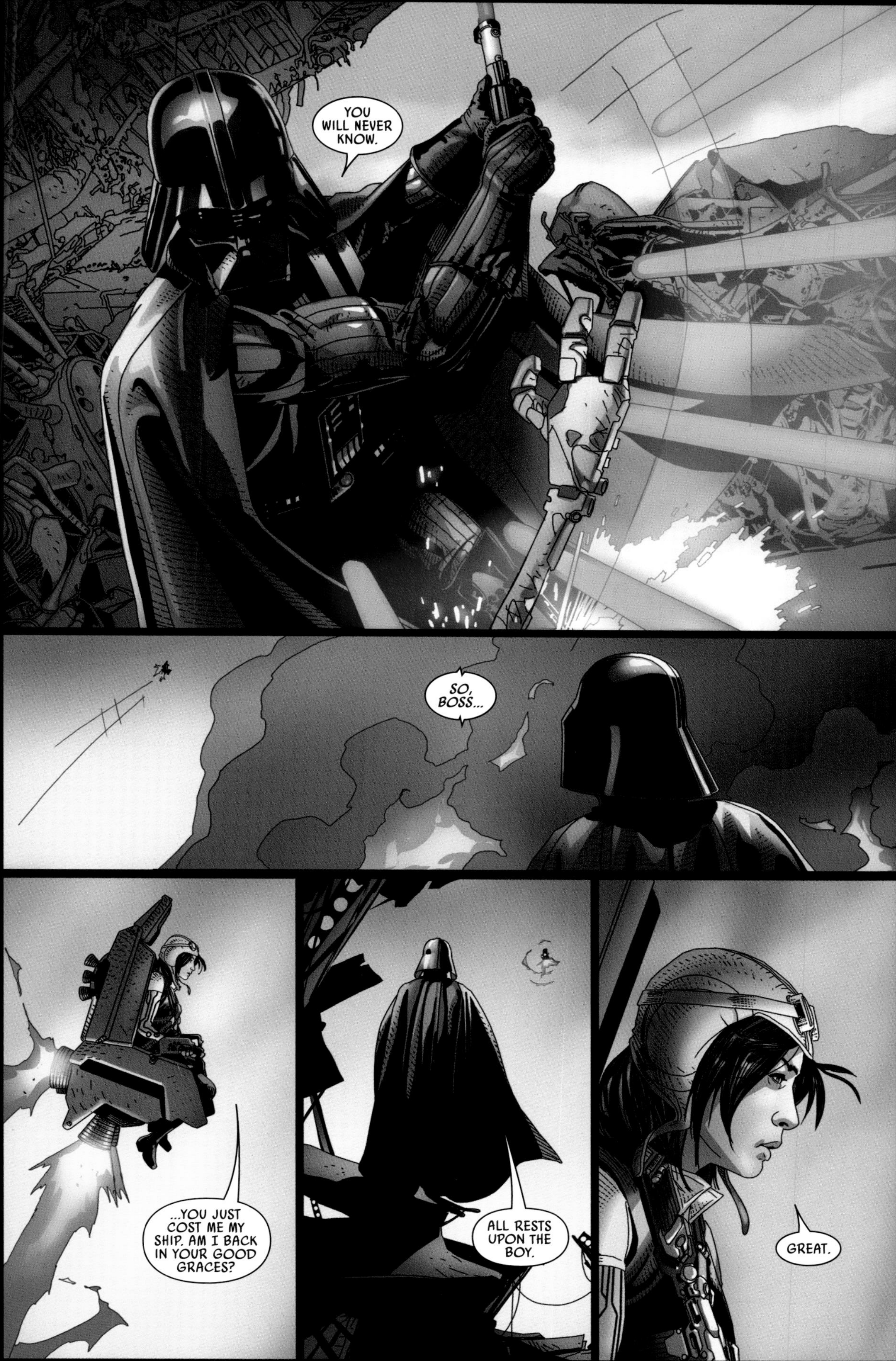
YOU WILL NEVER KNOW.
SO, BOSS...
...YOU JUST COST ME MY SHIP. AM I BACK IN YOUR GOOD GRACES?
ALL RESTS UPON THE BOY.
GREAT.

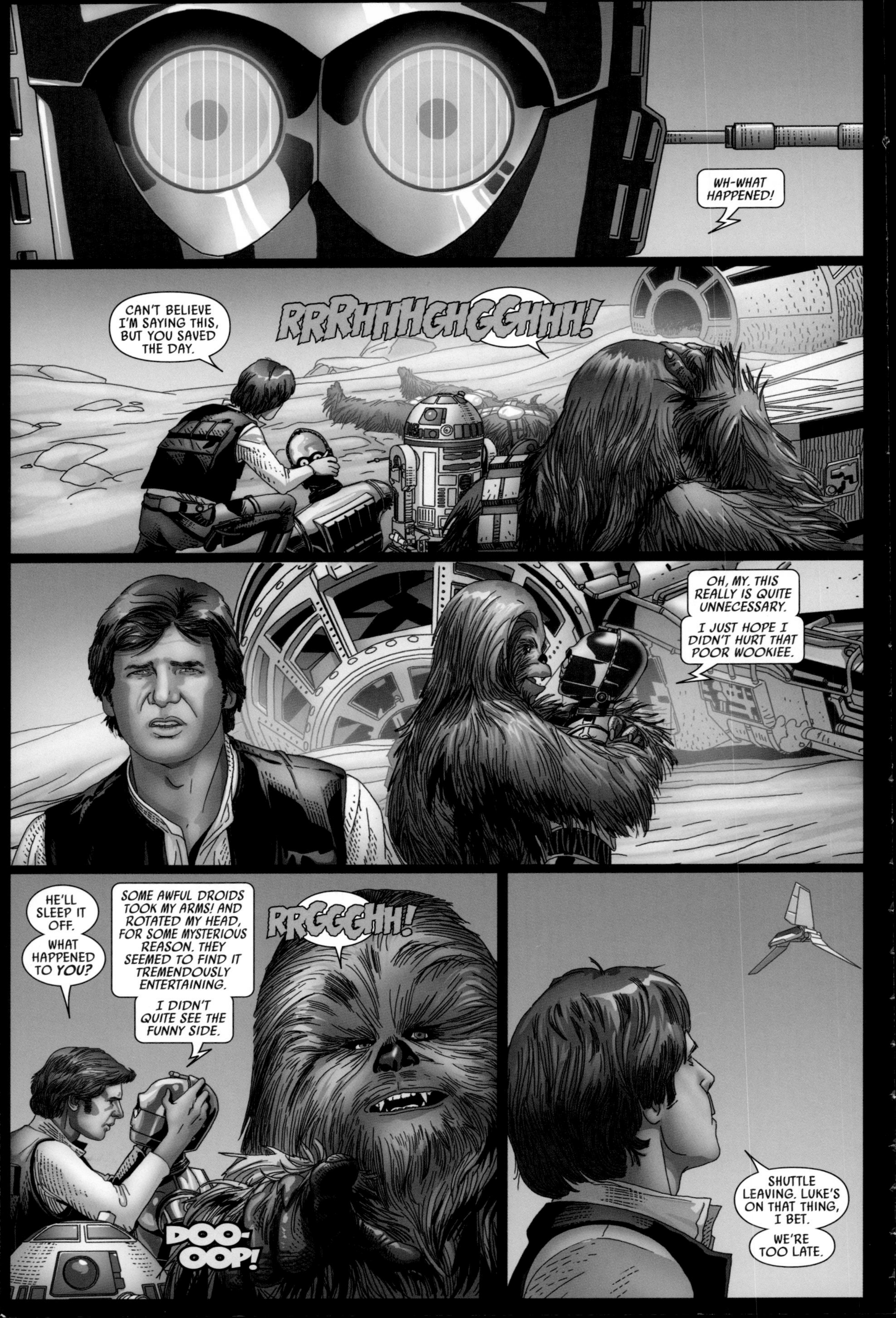
WH-WHAT HAPPENED!
CAN'T BELIEVE I'M SAYING THIS, BUT YOU SAVED THE DAY.
RRRHHHGHGGHHH!
OH, MY. THIS REALLY IS QUITE UNNECESSARY.
I JUST HOPE I DIDN'T HURT THAT POOR WOOKIEE.
HE'LL SLEEP IT OFF.
WHAT HAPPENED TO YOU?
SOME AWFUL DROIDS TOOK MY ARMS! AND ROTATED MY HEAD, FOR SOME MYSTERIOUS REASON. THEY SEEMED TO FIND IT TREMENDOUSLY ENTERTAINING.
I DIDN'T QUITE SEE THE FUNNY SIDE.
RRGGGHH!
DOO-OOP!
SHUTTLE LEAVING. LUKE'S ON THAT THING, I BET.
WE'RE TOO LATE.

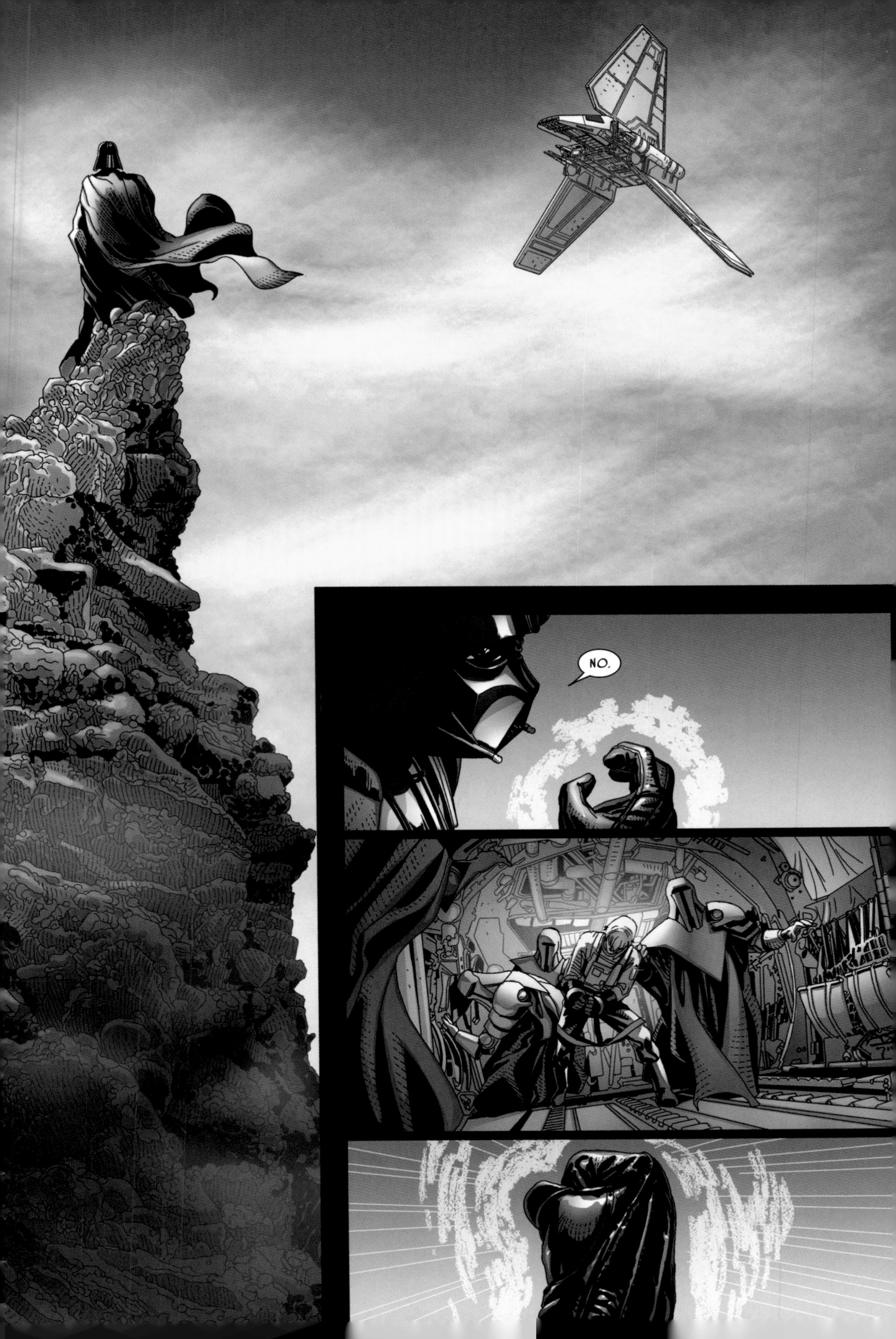
NO.

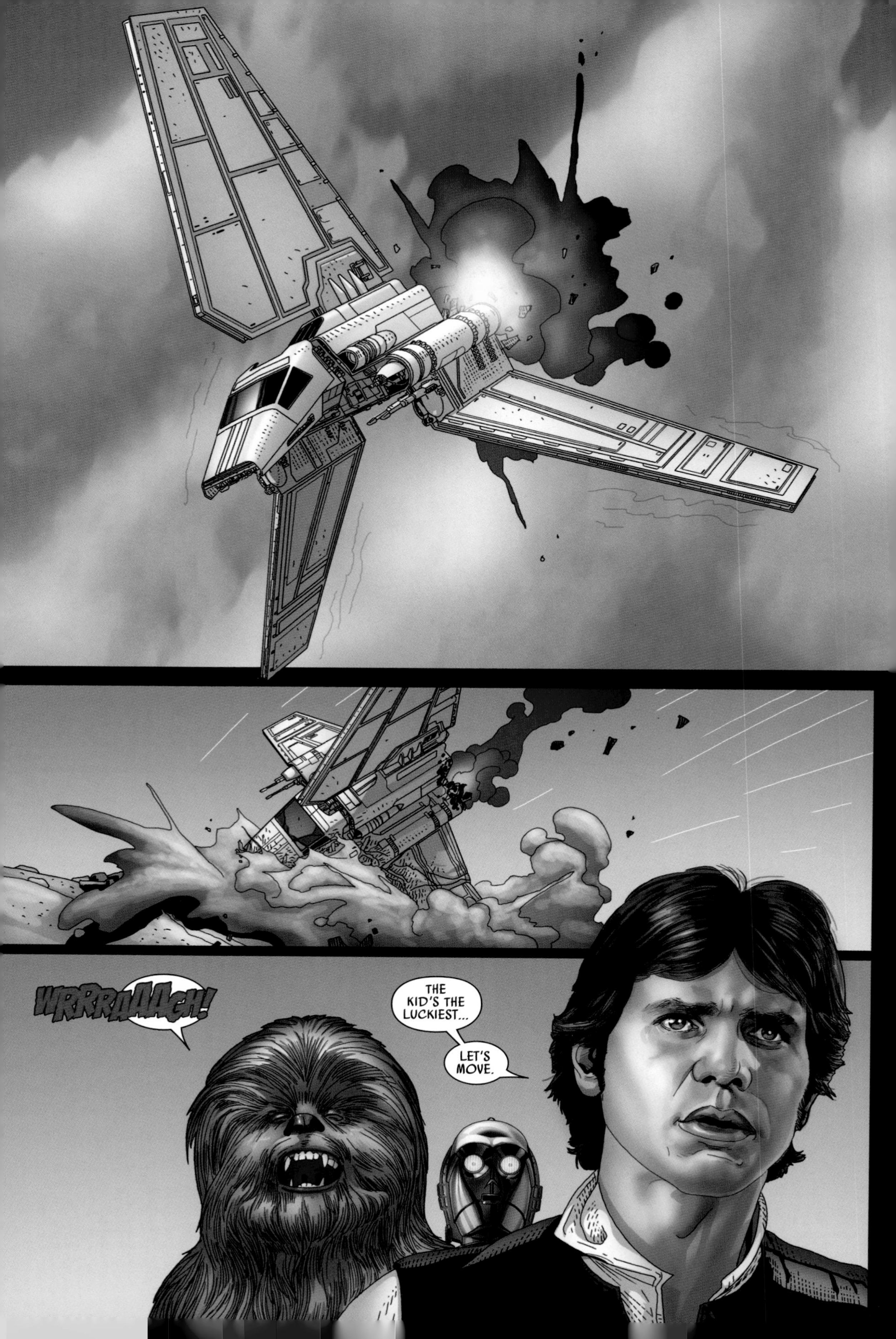
WRRRAAAAGH!
THE KID'S THE LUCKIEST...
LET'S MOVE.

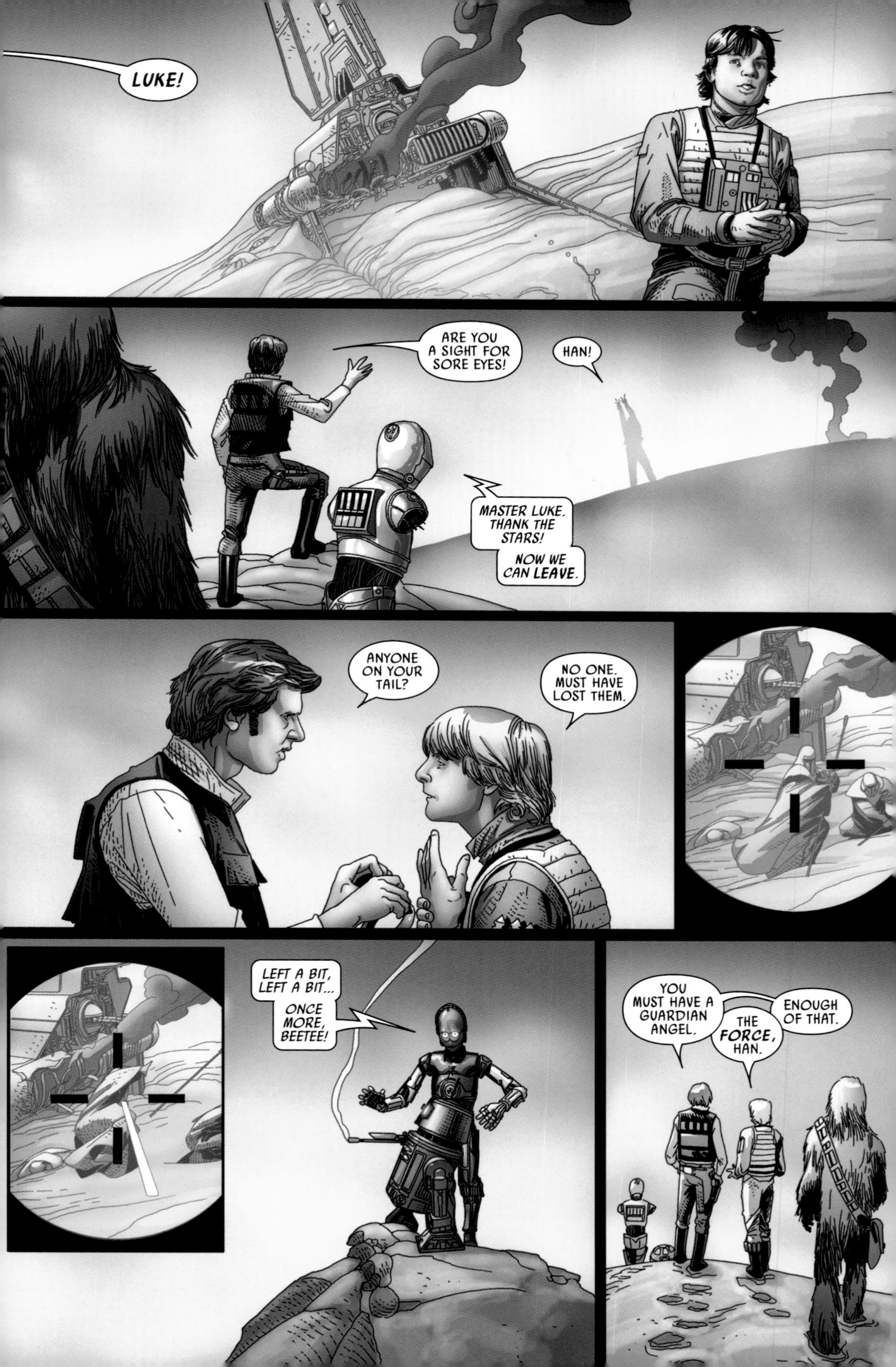
LUKE!
ARE YOU A SIGHT FOR SORE EYES!
HAN!
MASTER LUKE. THANK THE STARS!
NOW WE CAN LEAVE.
ANYONE ON YOUR TAIL?
NO ONE. MUST HAVE LOST THEM.
LEFT A BIT, LEFT A BIT...
ONCE MORE, BEETEE!
YOU MUST HAVE A GUARDIAN ANGEL.
THE FORCE, HAN.
ENOUGH OF THAT.

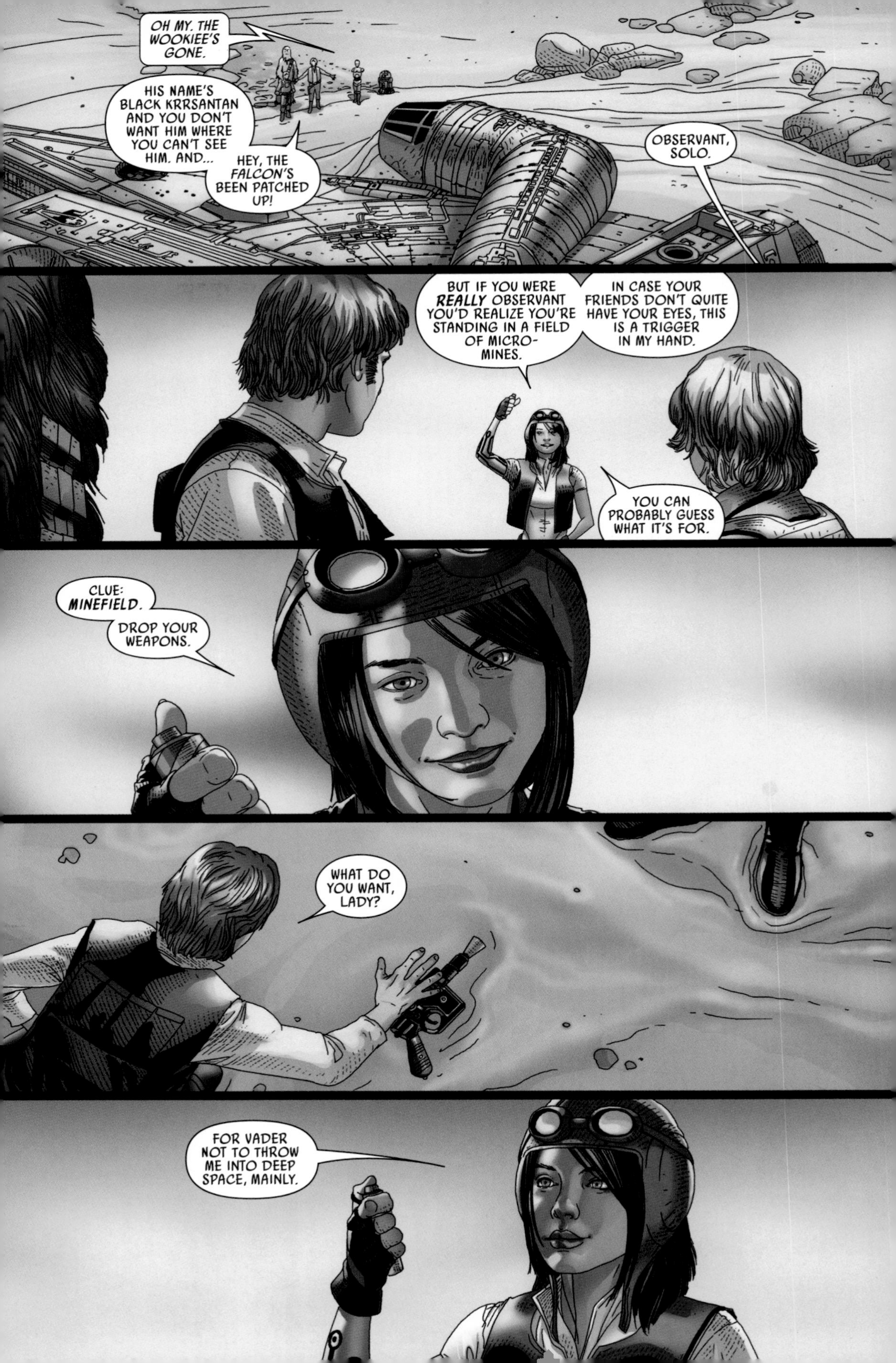
OH MY. THE WOOKIEE'S GONE.
HIS NAME'S BLACK KRRSANTAN AND YOU DON'T WANT HIM WHERE YOU CAN'T SEE HIM. AND...
HEY, THE FALCON'S BEEN PATCHED UP!
OBSERVANT, SOLO.
BUT IF YOU WERE REALLY OBSERVANT YOU'D REALIZE YOU'RE STANDING IN A FIELD OF MICRO-MINES.
IN CASE YOUR FRIENDS DON'T QUITE HAVE YOUR EYES, THIS IS A TRIGGER IN MY HAND.
YOU CAN PROBABLY GUESS WHAT IT'S FOR.
CLUE: MINEFIELD.
DROP YOUR WEAPONS.
WHAT DO YOU WANT, LADY?
FOR VADER NOT TO THROW ME INTO DEEP SPACE, MAINLY.

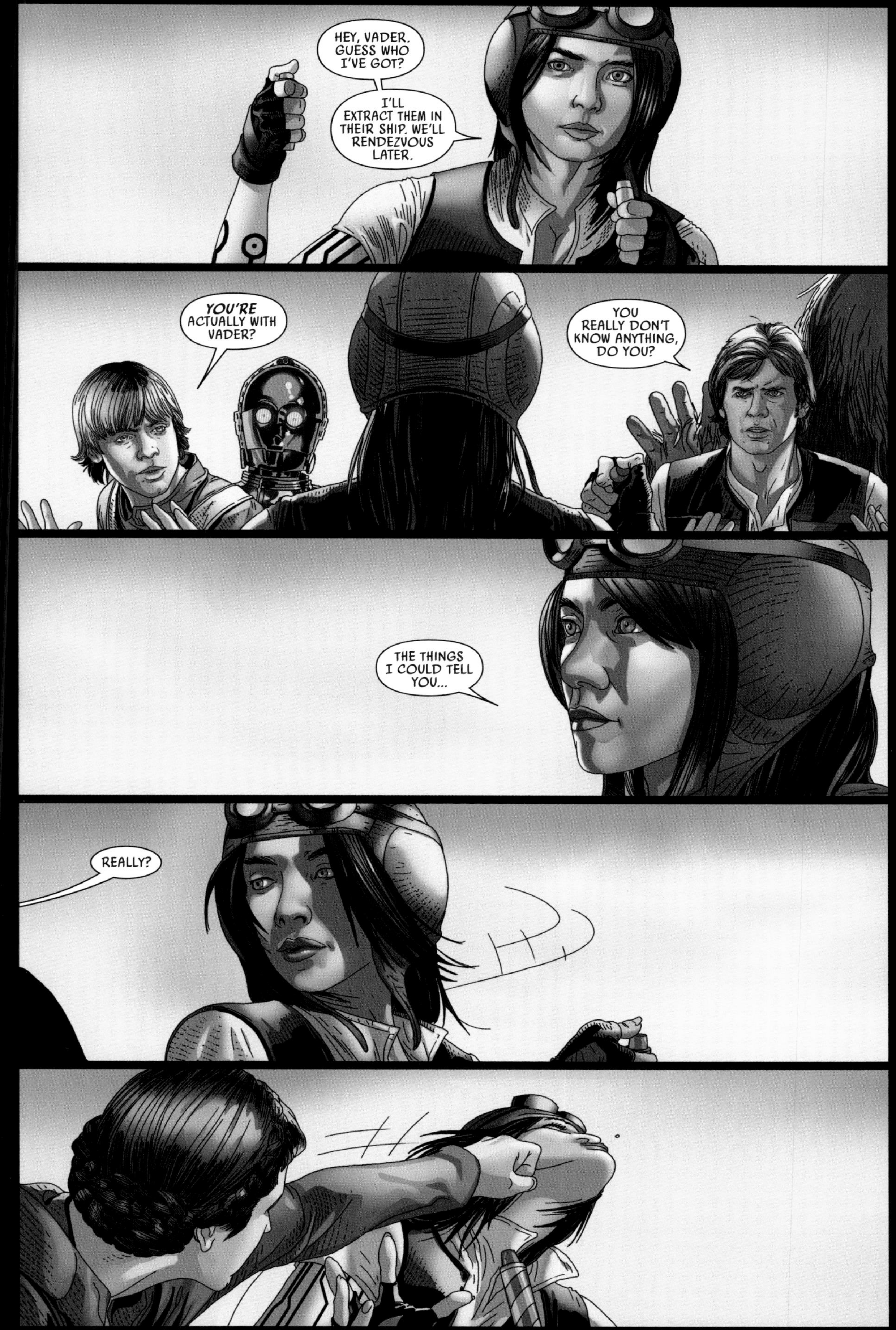
HEY, VADER. GUESS WHO I'VE GOT?
I'LL EXTRACT THEM IN THEIR SHIP. WE'LL RENDEZVOUS LATER.
YOU'RE ACTUALLY WITH VADER?
YOU REALLY DON'T KNOW ANYTHING, DO YOU?
THE THINGS I COULD TELL YOU...
REALLY?

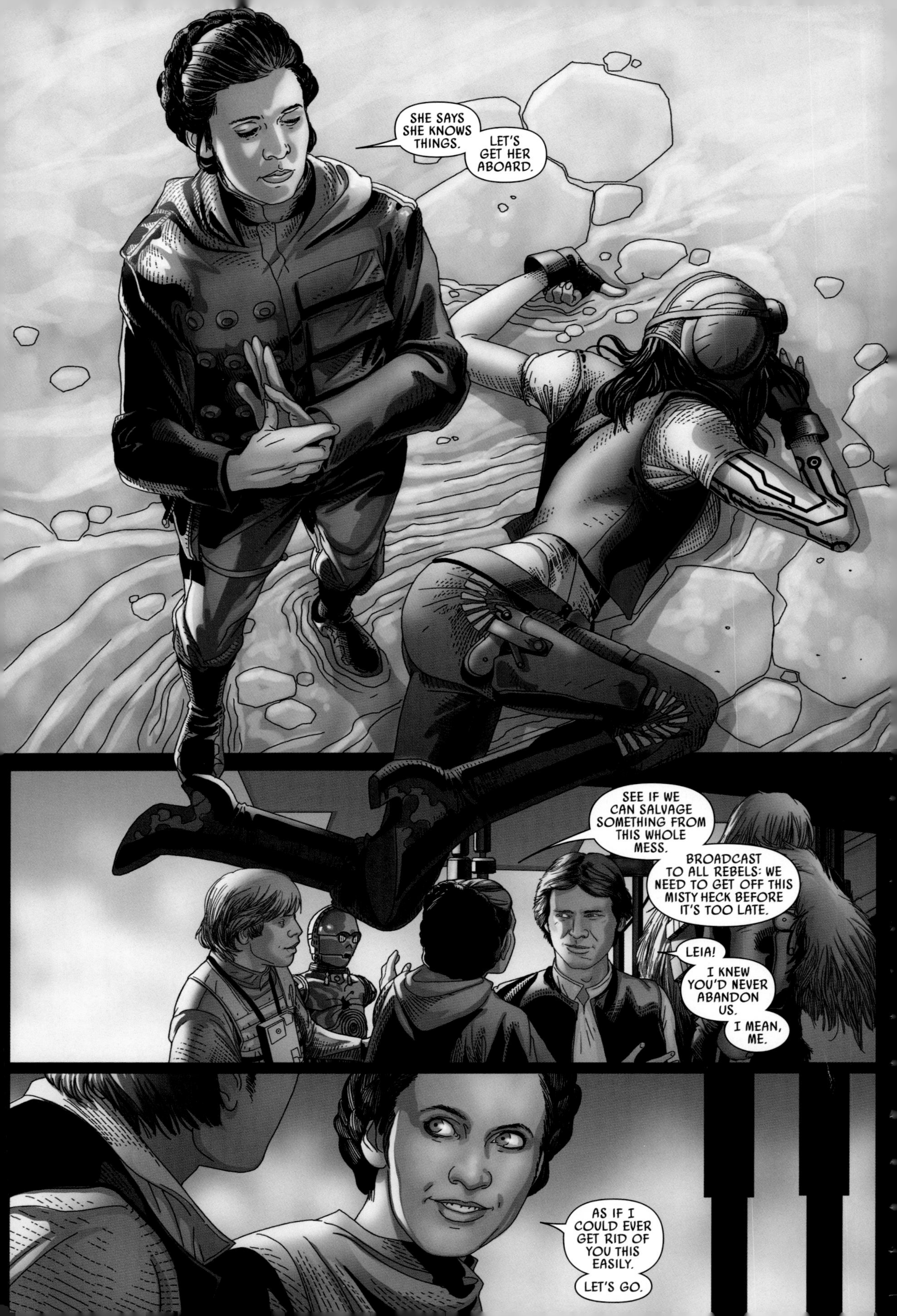
SHE SAYS SHE KNOWS THINGS.
LET'S GET HER ABOARD.
SEE IF WE CAN SALVAGE SOMETHING FROM THIS WHOLE MESS.
BROADCAST TO ALL REBELS: WE NEED TO GET OFF THIS MISTY HECK BEFORE IT'S TOO LATE.
LEIA!
I KNEW YOU'D NEVER ABANDON US.
I MEAN, ME.
AS IF I COULD EVER GET RID OF YOU THIS EASILY.
LET'S GO.

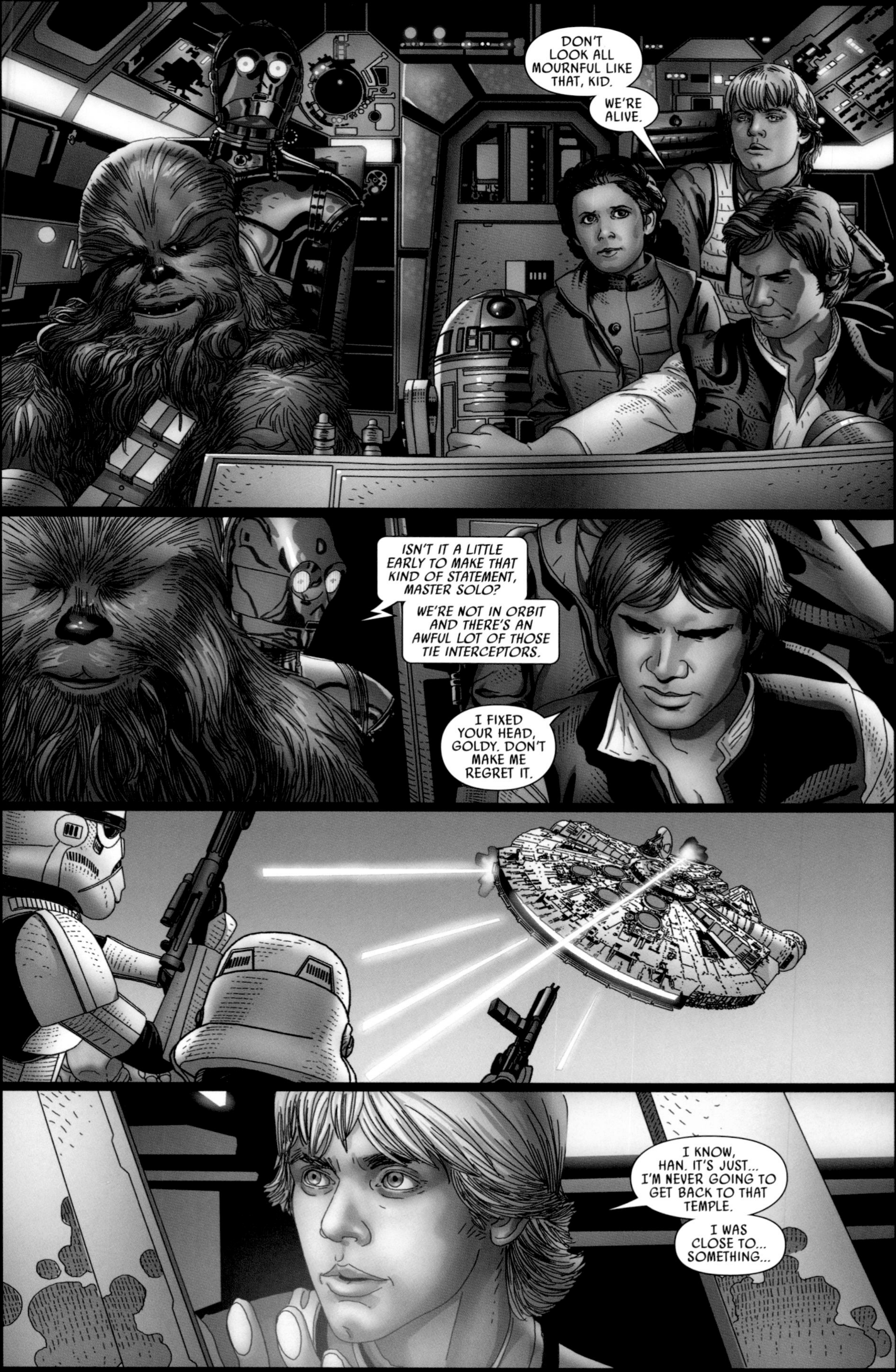
DON'T LOOK ALL MOURNFUL LIKE THAT, KID.
WE'RE ALIVE.
ISN'T IT A LITTLE EARLY TO MAKE THAT KIND OF STATEMENT, MASTER SOLO?
WE'RE NOT IN ORBIT AND THERE'S AN AWFUL LOT OF THOSE TIE INTERCEPTORS.
I FIXED YOUR HEAD, GOLDY. DON'T MAKE ME REGRET IT.
I KNOW, HAN. IT'S JUST... I'M NEVER GOING TO GET BACK TO THAT TEMPLE.
I WAS CLOSE TO... SOMETHING...

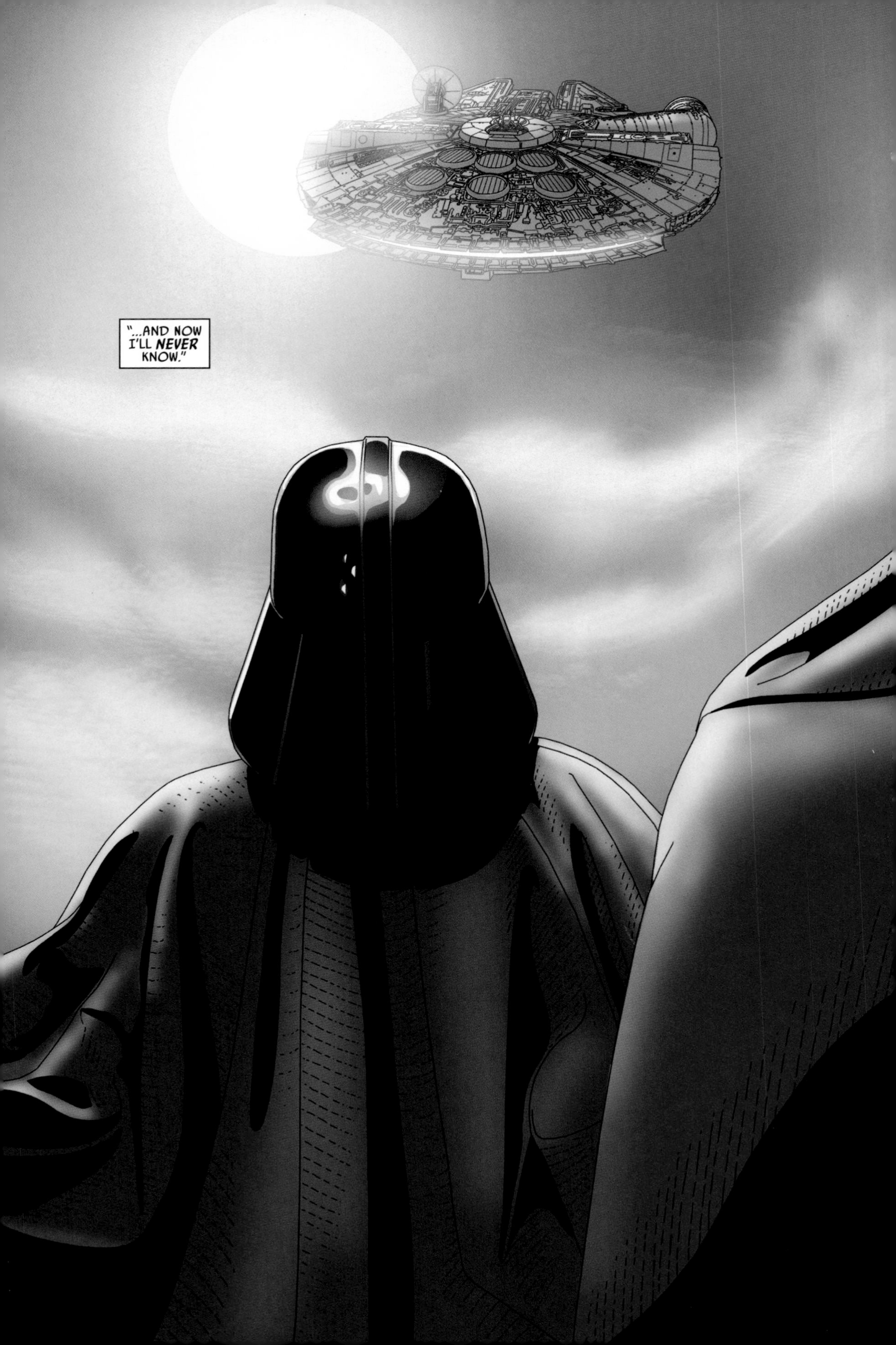
"...AND NOW I'LL NEVER KNOW."

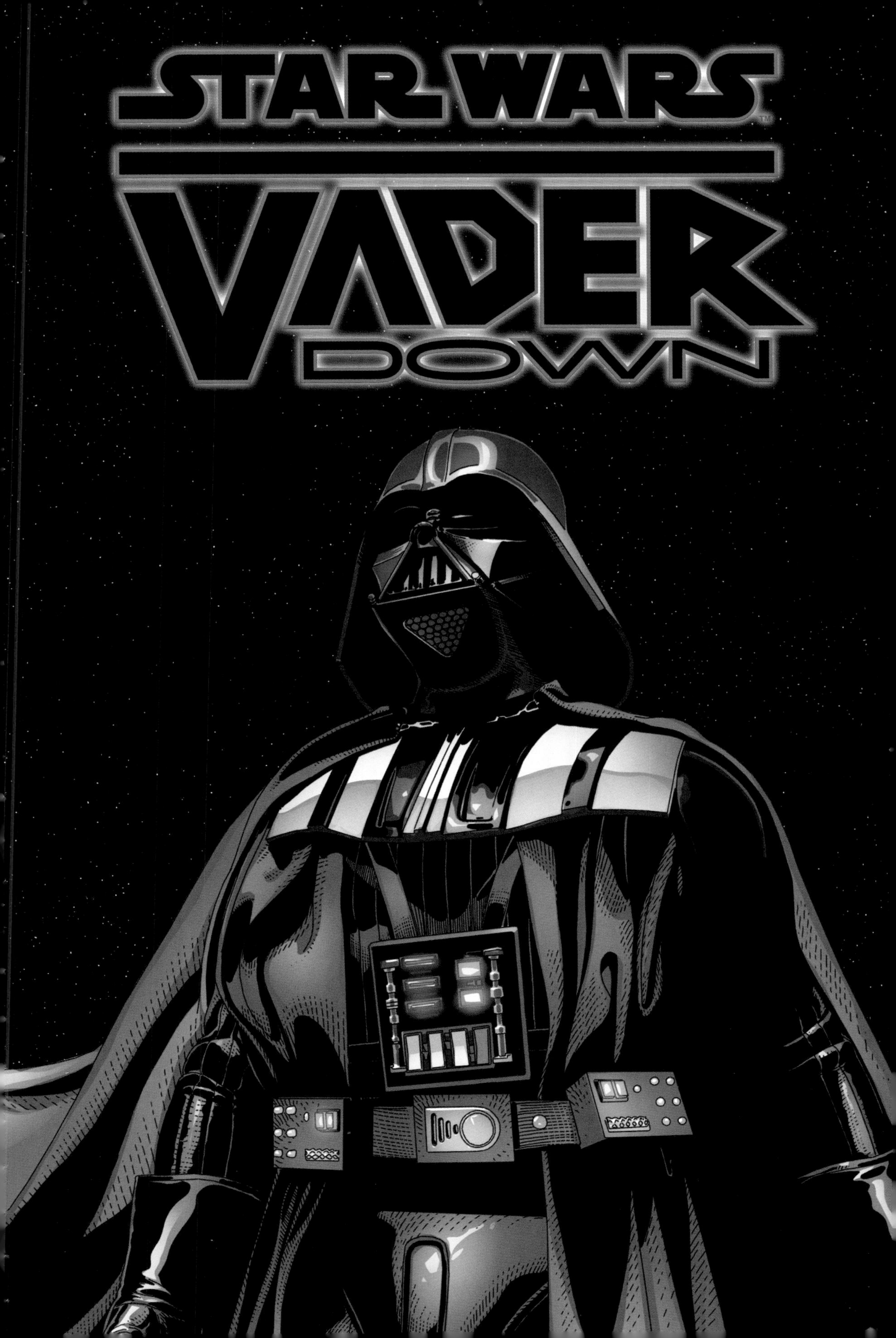

STAR WARS
VADER
DOWN

STAR WARS
VADER DOWN

COLLECT THEM ALL!

Set of 6 Hardcover Books ISBN: 978-1-61479-560-5

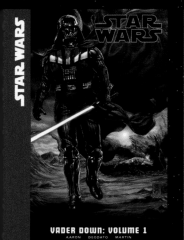

VADER DOWN: VOLUME 1
AARON   DEODATO   MARTIN

**Hardcover Book ISBN
978-1-61479-561-2**

VADER DOWN: VOLUME 2
GILLEN   LARROCA   DELGADO

**Hardcover Book ISBN
978-1-61479-562-9**

VADER DOWN: VOLUME 3
AARON   DEODATO   MARTIN

**Hardcover Book ISBN
978-1-61479-563-6**

VADER DOWN: VOLUME 4
GILLEN   LARROCA   DELGADO

**Hardcover Book ISBN
978-1-61479-564-3**

VADER DOWN: VOLUME 5
AARON   DEODATO   MARTIN

**Hardcover Book ISBN
978-1-61479-565-0**

VADER DOWN: VOLUME 6
GILLEN   LARROCA   DELGADO

**Hardcover Book ISBN
978-1-61479-566-7**